Julia Jones' Diary

My Secret Dream

Katrina Kahler

Table of Contents

Dream...

He looked at me and I truly thought my heart had skipped a beat. I'd never experienced that feeling before. But the sight of the new boy, Harry Robinson, walking in my direction and smiling warmly at me was something I had only dared to imagine.

"Do you want to dance?" he asked.

"Okay," I stammered. When he took hold of my hand and led me to the dance floor, I felt as if I were in heaven. "Is this really happening?" I wondered.

I could feel a familiar nervous anxiety starting to form in the pit of my stomach but his reassuring smile caused the uneasy feelings to completely disappear.

The image of the two of us, hand in hand as we danced to the slow romantic tune was etched in my mind. And as Sara Hamilton and her friends looked on with envy, I was the proudest 12 year old girl alive at that moment.

The sudden loud ringing in my ears was deafening as the image of Harry's handsome face quickly melted away. I opened my eyes and tried to focus. Then the realization hit me. I was actually in bed, my alarm was ringing and it was a school day. I had been dreaming.

"NOOO!" I cried. "That was the best dream ever! I want to go back to sleep and keep on dreaming!"

If only dreams did come true. This was the thought that flashed through my mind as I reluctantly tumbled out of bed and headed for the bathroom, only to find the door locked.

Great! Just what I need - my brother in the bathroom again. I swear that every time I want to use it, he seems to beat me.

And he's worse than me! For goodness sake, how can a boy take so long? I headed miserably downstairs for some breakfast.

"Aren't girls the ones who are supposed to hog bathrooms, not boys?" I asked my mother as I gulped down my cereal.

When my brother emerged, hair all gelled and reeking of after-shave, I was finally able to have my turn. With five minutes to spare, I stepped crossly over the dripping wet towel still lying in a pool of water on the floor and quickly got myself showered and ready for school.

Sitting on the school bus that morning, I thought back to the dream that I still remembered so vividly. Yes, if only dreams did come true! I would be the happiest girl ever!

But I knew that there was no way that was going to happen. Why on earth would a boy like Harry Robinson even look at me, let alone ask me to dance? Ever since starting at our school a few weeks ago, he had hung out in the popular crowd with the popular boys and the popular girls – the pretty girls. The group that I longed to be a part of but knew that I never would. I stared glumly out of the window as the bus pulled to a stop at the front of the school.

Friends...

"Hey Julia!" called Millie. I looked up to see my best friend running towards me, grinning from ear to ear. "You'll never guess what! Mom brought home a guitar last night. I mentioned that Mr. Casey is giving lessons at school and when I told her that I was keen to learn, she went out and bought one for me – just like that! It's so cool! And I'm going to start lessons this week."

"Wow!" I replied. "You're SO lucky!"

Learning the guitar was something that I'd wanted to do for ages now. But my parents weren't interested. "You have your dancing, Julia!" is what my mom always said when I asked her. "That's enough! Music lessons are very expensive and we can't afford for you to be taking up something else. Your dancing is enough!" she repeated. So I'd given up asking a long time ago.

I was happy for Millie but couldn't help feeling envious. Everything Millie wanted, Millie got. And she was even given things that she didn't want or hadn't asked for. She knew that I've been really keen to learn how to play guitar and now that we have a guitar teacher at school, it's the perfect opportunity. I've been talking to her about this for the last few weeks. But it now looks as though she's going to be the one learning and not me.

This happens a lot with Millie. She's a really good friend and everything, but it seems that she always gets what she wants. And she often gets the things I want as well. I guess if you have rich parents and they're happy to buy you things all the time, then why not?

The bell sounded and we headed off to class. I sat silently in my seat, thinking about Millie and how fortunate she was. I tried to convince myself not to be jealous but found it very difficult.

"You're quiet today!" Millie exclaimed at morning recess. "Is there something wrong?"

"No," I replied. "I'm fine. Just tired, that's all."

"Why don't you come over to my house this afternoon and I can show you my guitar?" Millie asked. "I'm sure you'll love it."

"Yes, I'm sure I will," I replied a little too sarcastically.

I then forced myself to snap out of it. I wasn't being fair to Millie. Just because she was rich and was often spoilt by her parents didn't give me the right to treat her badly. She was a good friend and didn't deserve that.

So I continued, "I'd love to come over, Millie. I'm sure Mom won't mind as long as I'm home by five."

We agreed that's what we would do and I proceeded to ask Millie about her guitar and what it looked like. As we sat there chatting, I spotted Harry Robinson and his friends, sitting in a group along with Sara Hamilton and some of her besties. Of course they were all together. They were the cool crowd. They didn't even notice kids like Millie and I. Although for this I was grateful.

Sara was new to our school last semester and I had been through a terrible time with her constantly bullying me. It had actually become so bad, that I had wanted to change schools. I'd had no idea that someone could be so mean. It was only because Miss Jennings, the school counselor, had helped me to be more assertive and confident, that I was able to stop the bullying from happening. It's amazing how effective it was when I simply stood up for myself rather than letting her bully me the way she did. And since then, she hasn't been a problem. Not to me anyway! I've noticed that she has since found other girls to pick on though.

I guess that some people are just like that. Miss Johnson said that people with low self-esteem often try to build themselves up by attempting to have control over others. That's certainly what Sara did to me. And looking back, I can't believe that I put up with it.

I'm so glad to be over that problem and while I really don't want to be Sara's friend, I would still like to hang out with the cool crowd. And Harry is so good looking! No wonder all those girls want to be near him. I sat there absentmindedly thinking about the dream I had had that morning.

Until Millie broke through my thoughts, "What are you thinking about Julia? You have a really strange look on your face!"

I turned bright red and looked away. I hadn't told Millie about my crush on Harry and especially that I had been dreaming about him. That was just too embarrassing!

Imagine if she told the other kids. And imagine if Harry found out. How humiliating that would be! I'd be the laughing stock of the whole of grade seven. Sara Hamilton and all her friends would think it was hilarious. No, I had already decided, that it was best to keep things like that to myself.

And besides that, Millie isn't very good at keeping secrets. Last year, she told Kristy Richards that I didn't like her. I can't believe she did that. Sure it was true that I didn't like Kristy Richards. She was really possessive of Millie and wouldn't let me anywhere near her. Every time I tried to join in, she would take Millie in the opposite direction and leave me out. But I didn't want Millie to tell her what I had said. Kristy ended up bursting into tears, I got into trouble from the teacher for being mean to her and she hasn't spoken to me since.

I wish I could tell Millie secrets though. Isn't that what best friends are for? But Millie has changed a lot lately. I know that she wants to be part of the cool group too. And sometimes, I think that she'd rather be friends with them than with me.

Some of those kids are learning guitar with Mr. Casey. He's a really cool teacher and really popular with all the kids at our school. I'm wondering if that's why Millie wants to learn, so she can become one of the cool kids and they'll accept her into their group.

But I didn't want to think about that happening. That would be terrible. So I switched my thoughts back to our plans for the afternoon. Then before I knew it, I was laughing with Millie and having fun, the way I usually did when we were together. It was so nice to be completely oblivious of everyone else, including Harry Robinson; just Millie and I, hanging out and being best friends. I decided there was no way that anything could affect our friendship.

I want to be a Rock Star...

"Millie's guitar is so cool!" I thought to myself as I lay in bed, trying to drift off to sleep. Our afternoon together at her house had been fun, the way I knew it would be. It always is when it's just Millie and I together, with no one else around to distract or bother us.

When Millie offered me a turn, I couldn't resist and before I knew it, I had figured out how to play a simple song. "That's amazing," Millie had commented. "Who showed you how to do that?"

"No one," I replied. "I just kind of figured it out by myself."

"Julia, you're a natural," Millie had said. "You're the one who really should be learning how to play."

I tossed and turned, Millie's words racing through my head. I would desperately love to learn how to play the guitar. People have commented many times that I have music in my blood. I love dancing and I guess I'm pretty good at that. But I love listening to music and singing, just as much. I often go on YouTube to learn the words to the latest hit songs. Apparently, my great grandmother was some type of classical singer, so maybe I get it from her. The problem is that neither of my parents are into music at all, so they're not interested whatsoever in encouraging me in that direction.

"You need to focus on your school work, Julia! Stop that daydreaming and get your homework done!" That's the most important thing in my mother's mind. Well as far as I'm concerned, there's definitely more to life than schoolwork! There's dancing and playing guitar and Harry Robinson and…

I rolled over for what seemed like the hundredth time and told myself to stop thinking about things I can't have.

"You're such a dreamer, Julia!" Mom had said while sitting at the dinner table earlier in the evening. "You need to learn to be realistic and accept that there are things you can have and things you can't. Now finish eating and go upstairs so you can get your homework done!"

She hadn't been at all interested in hearing about Millie's guitar or the fact that we have a really cool new guitar teacher at school that everyone seems to be going to for lessons…all the cool kids, anyway.

Apparently Mr. Casey is even talking about forming a band with some of his students. That would be so awesome!

I lay there, visions floating through my head of being on stage, playing guitar and singing, while Harry Robinson stood in the crowd, his adoring eyes following my every move.

Maybe I do need to be realistic, but my dreams are mine and no one can take that away from me! That was my final thought as I eventually drifted off to sleep.

Stop daydreaming, Julia...

At school the next day, everyone was talking about learning guitar. A few of the kids in our class have already had lessons and have been raving about how good they are.

Apparently Mr. Casey teaches the songs that his students want to learn, including all the iTunes hits that everyone loves. We used to have a different guitar teacher but he wasn't very popular because he taught heaps of classical and old school stuff that no one knew. And that would have been pretty boring I guess. But the new teacher is really different. Now, heaps of people are keen to sign up for lessons. Mr. Casey teaches other instruments as well and several kids are hoping to form a band.

Millie goes for her first lesson tomorrow and she's really excited about it. I'm excited for her too, but I still feel jealous. If only there was a way that I could get a guitar. It was all I could think about (apart from Harry Robinson) and I found it really hard to concentrate in class.

"Julia Jones!" screeched Mrs. Jackson, our teacher. "Can you please answer my question?" I quickly turned towards her, turning bright red.

"Umm!" was all I could reply. I had no idea what she was

talking about or even what her question was. Everyone stared at me and laughed.

"She's day dreaming again," called out Zane Woodford, a loud-mouthed kid who sits at the back and thinks he's really good. That comment just made everyone laugh even harder. I looked at Millie who was staring at me sympathetically, but there was obviously nothing that she could do.

"See me after class, Julia!" demanded Mrs. Jackson. "I think we need to have a talk. And perhaps I also need to call your parents."

"Great!" I thought to myself. "That's all I need! As if Mom isn't nagging me enough about school work already."

I decided then to make a bigger effort and try to concentrate more. I certainly didn't want Mrs. Jackson calling Mom or Dad. Thankfully, this tactic seemed to pay off because when I stayed to see Mrs. Jackson after school, she commented on how much better my concentration level had been during the afternoon. She then simply told me to make sure that it continued.

On the bus ride home after school, I sat with my friend, Blake Jansen, who I used to have a crush on. Millie was always saying that he liked me and tried to convince me to start going out with him.

But I think he was too shy for that and besides, it was nice just hanging out with him as a friend. And then Harry Robinson arrived at our school. That changed everything!

Some of the girls and boys in our class are going out together and Millie is always saying that she wants a boyfriend too. Yesterday, she even mentioned Harry. I can't believe that she likes him as well! So typical – it's as if everything I want Millie also seems to want, but the trouble is that she often gets it!

As the bus headed along the route towards my house, I chatted with Blake and told him about wanting to learn how to play guitar. He thought that was really cool. Blake is actually a drummer and has been learning since he was pretty young. His dad is a drummer and taught him how to play. His whole family is really musical and they even have a special sound-proof room where Blake can practice. He's so lucky.

We talked about music and our favorite bands and it made me realize how much Blake and I have in common. Since the last holidays, I had hardly seen Blake and it was really nice to hang out with him again.

We were so busy chatting that I almost missed my stop. When I hopped off the bus, for the first time since he arrived at our school, Harry Robinson was the furthest thing from my mind. And for some reason, I suddenly felt happier than I had in ages. With a smile on my face, I opened my front door, thinking that maybe things weren't so bad after all!

The Book…

The first thing that caught my eye as I entered the house was an unusual looking book. It had been left on the hallway stand next to the front door. This was where Mom and Dad usually put their car keys and the mail as they walked inside. And we all hung our coats on the brass hooks that were attached to the framework.

Usually, I headed straight for the kitchen when I arrived home in the afternoons, as I was always desperately hungry and wanted something to eat. But something about the unfamiliar book made me stop and pick it up.

The gold swirly letters of the title seemed to jump right out at me but it was the actual name of the book that made me gasp. "How to Make Your Dreams Come True." It seemed as if this book had been left there especially for me and that I was definitely meant to read it.

Almost trance like, I headed for the stairs and the quiet solitude of my bedroom. Completely forgetting how hungry I was, I dropped my school bag on the floor and sat down excitedly on my bed. I usually do enjoy reading but within minutes, I was totally absorbed and before I knew it, several hours had passed and Mom was calling me downstairs for dinner.

Reluctantly, I left the book open on my bed and raced to the dinner table hoping to finish dinner quickly so that I could get back to reading where I had left off, as soon as possible.

"I haven't seen you all afternoon, Julia. Do you have lots of homework?" Mom asked.

"Yes, I do have a bit," I replied, "but I found a really

interesting book on the hallway stand. Where did it come from?"

I looked at my mother waiting curiously for her answer. "An old friend turned up on our doorstep this morning," answered Mom. "It was completely unexpected. She was lucky to catch me at home."

"Who was it?" I asked.

"Mary Johnson, an old friend from way back. You've never met her before, but she's visiting the area and thought she'd drop in to see me."

"I remember her!" said Dad. "She was always a bit weird, a bit hippy like, into alternative types of thinking."

"Yes, she was and she hasn't changed a bit," said Mom. "She left that book for me. She said that she thought I should read it."

"Well, do you mind if I read it? It looks really interesting." I commented. I didn't dare tell her that I had been reading it all afternoon and was almost finished. That would just be inviting trouble!

As I expected, she replied, "As long as you get your homework done first."

"Okay," I replied, smiling inside. "I'd better get moving then, so I can get it all done."

"I'll do the dishes tonight, Julia," said Dad. "You go up and get stuck into your school work." He winked discreetly at me and then continued eating his meal.

"Thanks so much, Dad. You're the best!" I replied gratefully. And before Mom could argue, I quickly excused myself from the table and raced back upstairs.

With my brother away on school camp, it was up to me to get all the chores done. I was so happy that Dad had offered to help me out and I couldn't get back to my room quickly enough.

The book was like nothing I'd ever read before and a couple of hours later I had finished it. I felt so disappointed that it had come to an end.

As I got ready for bed, my head was filled with ideas and thoughts that had never occurred to me before. What if I really can make my dreams come true? What if the ideas in this book really do work?

My mind was racing as I hopped under the covers, way too alert to even think about sleeping yet. I lay there restlessly, my head spinning with visions of guitars, singing on stage, and Harry Robinson's handsome face.

How to Make Your Dreams Come True, it's the most inspiring book I think I've ever read! Smiling, I rolled over and closed my eyes, wondering what tomorrow would bring.

A change in thinking...

During the bus ride to school, I thought about the mysterious book. I was convinced that I had found it for a reason and was determined to take on board all the ideas that I had read about.

I recalled the main messages that the book described so clearly. It was all about being positive and having a positive mindset. Rather than constantly having negative thoughts and worrying about things all the time, which just makes you more upset and more worried, it's much better to focus on good things happening.

There were lots of stories in the book of people actually making their dreams come true by having positive thoughts. And suddenly, it all seemed to make sense. If I started really believing that I can have the things I dream about, then maybe my dreams will come true. Rather than being negative and constantly thinking bad thoughts, if I change my thoughts to positive ones, who knows what I could create? I decided that it was definitely worth a try and that I had absolutely nothing to lose!

"What are you looking so happy about?" Millie asked as I stepped off the bus. "You have a huge smile on your face! What's going on? Tell me!" she urged as we walked to class together.

"I don't know," I replied. "I read this really interesting book last night and it's all about having a positive attitude and making your dreams come true. So I thought I'd give it a try. And do you know what? Just deciding to be positive about things instantly makes me feel happy."

"You're weird sometimes, Julia," Millie sighed. "Sometimes,

I have no idea what you're talking about."

I ignored her comment and opened my Math book, ready to start work. When Mrs. Jackson gave us our homework assignment later that morning, familiar groans could be heard throughout the classroom. But rather than complaining along with everyone else, the way I usually did, I smiled. Then I pictured myself with my homework assignment completed and a beautiful big A written in the top right hand corner.

Grinning, I walked out of the room with Millie and headed downstairs for morning recess.

Envy...

"Oh my gosh, that was amazing!" Millie beamed as she literally skipped down the hallway after her first guitar lesson that afternoon. I had been waiting outside for her to finish, as we'd planned to go back to her house after school.

"I could hear you playing," I commented. "It sounded like you did really well for your first lesson!"

"Mr. Casey is so nice! He showed me how to play some basic chords and soon I'll be able to start playing songs. I told him who my favorite singers are and he's going to work out an easy version of their songs so I'll be able to play them."

"That will be so much fun," I replied. "You'll have to show me what you've learnt when we get to your house."

Millie's mom was waiting in her car just outside the school gates and was very pleased to hear that Millie had enjoyed her lesson so much.

"I was a bit apprehensive, Julia," she said to me as we drove along. "Millie has a bad habit of starting things but not following through. I hope that she wants to keep these lessons going. It'll mean lots of practice, Millie."

Millie rolled her eyes at her mother and then said adamantly, "Of course I'll practice Mom. That was the deal, remember? And besides, this is really fun, so of course I'll want to practice!"

Millie's mom didn't look convinced but then a thought seemed to occur to her. "You should learn guitar too, Julia. Then you girls could practice together."

"I'd love to learn, Mrs. Spencer," I replied, "but I don't have a guitar."

"Why don't you ask your parents if they'll buy you one?" Mrs. Spencer seemed to think that's all there was to it. But then she added, "When's your birthday? You never know what might show up!"

"My mother isn't keen on me learning," I said. "She thinks that my dancing is enough."

"Well, you just don't know what the future holds, Julia. If you really want something, just focus on it happening, and you never know."

Mrs. Spencer's comment struck me with a thud. Millie ignored her and rolled her eyes once more, then started prattling on about a new dress that she wanted.

But all I could think about was what Mrs. Spencer had said. Out of the blue, an idea started to form in my mind and I quietly filed it away to concentrate on later, when I was on my own and had time to think.

We spent the afternoon in Millie's room. It seemed to me that Millie chose to see her guitar as if it were a new toy that she wanted to show off and after a few minutes of trying to play what she had learnt, she put it down.

"This is boring," she said, "Let's do something else."

"Can I have a quick go?" I asked, hopefully.

The sight of that beautiful gleaming new guitar was just too much. I had to have a turn. The afternoon sun glinted on the shiny blue lacquer. It was such a pretty color and I couldn't help but feel envious. Millie was so lucky!

Mr. Casey had convinced Millie's mom that she should buy her an electric guitar as it's so much easier to learn on than an acoustic. And she even had a small amplifier to go with it. Millie was more than happy with this choice as she thought the other kids would think it was cool. I turned the knob to adjust the volume and my strumming gave off a crisp clear sound.

"Please teach me what you learnt today," I begged.

"Oh, alright!" she complained and abruptly took the guitar from me to demonstrate what she had been taught.

"I can't really remember but I think it goes like this," Millie wasn't completely sure and the sound that emanated was quite distorted and off key. After handing the guitar back to me, it was only a matter of minutes before I had figured out what she'd been attempting to play. And I strummed the chords with little difficulty whatsoever.

"That's enough," she said crossly, quickly taking the guitar from me. "Let's do something else. I know, I'll show you the new dress Mom bought for me yesterday."

So we spent the remainder of the afternoon looking through Millie's wardrobe and I ended up going home with some things that Millie never wore any more.

"You may as well have these," she said. "They just sit in my wardrobe and they're practically brand new. It's such a waste if they're not worn."

I gratefully accepted the clothes. She really was very generous sometimes and I felt glad to have something new to wear.

When my dad came to pick me up later, I couldn't help but tell him all about Millie's new guitar. I knew that he would at least listen to what I had to say and not just interrogate me about my progress at school, the way Mom always did.

He listened quietly and commented that yes, Millie was a very lucky girl. Then switched the subject to dancing and asked me how that was going. I do love dancing and I would never want to give it up but I now seem to be more and more obsessed with the thought of having my own guitar and learning how to play.

As I climbed the stairs to my bedroom, I thought about the Dreams book sitting on my bedside table and reminded myself of my vow to remain positive.

Then Mrs. Spencer's words suddenly came into my head…"If you really want something, just focus on it happening."

So I stretched out on my bed, closed my eyes, and for the next ten minutes I created images in my mind of myself as a great guitarist. The best part was that I could feel the joy inside me absolutely bubbling over.

My brother...

I spent Saturday morning at my dance class, something I always looked forward to. Then that afternoon, I decided that I had better complete my homework assignment that was due on Monday. This particular project was all Math, something I don't really enjoy because I find it hard.

But I had already decided that I was going to have a positive attitude. So once more, I focused on creating a picture in my head of being given back my homework assignment with a big red A written in bold letters in the top right hand corner.

I always have to work really hard in Math, but this time I'd love to do well. So before attempting to begin, I sat for a few minutes thinking about what I wanted to happen and felt really good about it. I pictured myself with a massive smile on my face, showing my mom my result.

It was amazing, because just doing that one thing made me keen to get started. Normally I put complicated things off until the last minute, but I could feel that having the right attitude was going to make my assignment much easier to complete.

To my huge surprise when I looked at the clock a little later, 2 hours had passed but I had barely noticed the time. By this stage, I was almost finished and feeling very pleased. It was quite strange, but I was convinced that the positive attitude that I had taken on board was really helping me to get through my homework. Then I read the last question, the question that would get me an A if I were able to complete it.

My heart sank as I realized that I had no idea how to do it. I decided to call Millie to see if she could help, but to my disappointment, she wasn't at home. Then, just as I was about to give up, my brother walked into my room.

"What are you up to, sis?" His friendly approach could only mean one thing. He wanted something! I swear that it's the only time he's nice to me!

I could see that he was freshly showered, his hair was all gelled and he reeked of Dad's after-shave. I have no idea why my brother wears that stuff. He doesn't even have to shave yet!

He sat down on my bed and pretended that he was interested in what I was doing. All of sudden an idea occurred to me. "Hey, Matt!" I said to him, "Do you think you could help me out with this one Math question? I'm really stuck and I have no idea how to do it!"

"Oh Julia, I have to meet the guys in half an hour!" he groaned. "Why don't you ask Mom or Dad to help you?"

"They're out for the afternoon," I replied. "And I promised Mom that I'd have this finished by the time she gets home. Otherwise, I'm not allowed to go to Millie's for a sleep over tonight."

"Well," he said, "I'll make a deal. I'll help you with this only if you lend me your iPod docking station. It's Karl's birthday party this afternoon and his isn't working. He's freaking out because he won't be able to play any music."

Mom and Dad had bought the docking station for my birthday and ever since, Matt was always asking if he could borrow it. It was probably the only time he was ever nice to me! But this time, I decided to use it to my advantage. Whenever I asked him for help with homework in the past, it was always a flat out, "No! I'm too busy!" But I was counting on this time being different.

I must admit that I never like him borrowing my stuff. Mainly because I'm worried that he won't look after it. But this was the answer to my problem, so I reluctantly agreed.

Then before long, he had helped me to figure out the last tricky question and my assignment was done. I felt overjoyed and once more, pictured that beautiful, big, red A in my head.

Just as Matt was about to leave, my docking station tucked carefully under his arm, I couldn't help but ask, "So, is Lily going to the party this afternoon?"

He immediately turned bright red, which was a complete give away. "Aaah, I'm not sure," he stammered. "Anyway, I've got to go, or I'll be late. See ya!"

And with that he was gone.

I knew that he was going out with Lily. His friend, Karl had let it slip when he was hanging out at our house one afternoon. But Matt didn't know that I knew. Ever since he started grade 8, he's been acting really weird. He never used to care what he looked like but now he always takes forever in the bathroom and goes through bucket loads of hair gel.

Mom said it's probably his hormones taking over. Well, I know what it really is. It's Lily Thompson, that's what!

Mom would probably freak out if she knew he had a girlfriend. Our mom is so old-fashioned. So many kids our age have girlfriends and boyfriends but Mom says we have to wait until we're older. In the meantime, schoolwork is all that matters.

Dad's a bit more lenient, but he doesn't get much of a say. Usually whatever Mom says, everyone has to do, including Dad.

I decided to put all those thoughts from my mind and concentrated on getting my things together to go to Millie's. We'd been planning this sleep over all week and I couldn't wait to have another turn on her guitar. I'd even found some simple guitar lessons on YouTube and was hoping to try them out at her place if she lets me. It was going to be heaps of fun and I couldn't wait to get there.

Left out…

I arrived at Millie's house at 5pm, which was what we had arranged at school the day before. However, when her mom opened the door, she looked surprised to see me.

"Julia, how are you?" she asked in her usual friendly manner. "Millie isn't home yet. I thought you weren't arriving until later."

She must have seen the confused look on my face because she quickly added, "Oh, I'm sure she'll be home soon. She's just at the mall looking for a present for her dad's birthday. You can go on up to her room and wait for her there. You're bound to find plenty to do."

"Thanks, Mrs. Spencer," I replied. "Do you think Millie would mind if I played her guitar? I'll be really careful with it," I reassured her.

"Oh, that's absolutely fine. I'm sure Millie won't mind," she answered. "To be honest with you, she's hardly touched it. I was hoping that her enthusiasm would last longer than a week, at least. It'll be good to see it being used."

Eagerly, I raced up to Millie's room and carefully removed her guitar from its case. The shiny, blue lacquer glimmered once more and the feel of it in my hands gave me an instant thrill. I strummed a few chords, trying to remember the lessons I had viewed on YouTube. Then I spotted Millie's open laptop on her desk.

She was logged onto Facebook and just as I was about to get up a new tab so I could look for the guitar lessons that I'd found at home earlier, something caught my eye. It appeared that Millie had lots of Facebook friends and a couple of names instantly jumped out at me. I stared open-mouthed in shock as I read the recent posts on display…

"Who wants to hang out at the mall this afternoon?" was the first comment, followed by Millie's eager reply.

What shocked me the most were the names that were staring out from her computer screen.

Millie was in a conversation with Harry Robinson, Sara Hamilton and several other kids from their group. And they had all been planning to go to the mall together that afternoon. Then I saw a picture that made my jaw drop. Millie was tagged in it and the photo had the caption, "Besties!"

I felt my stomach churn as I quickly exited the page and moved away from the computer, Millie's guitar lying forgotten on her bed. I knew that I had done the wrong thing.

Looking at Millie's Facebook was completely wrong and I was riddled with guilt for invading her privacy. But what bothered me the most was that Millie was hanging out with that group behind my back. I thought of the occasions recently when Millie had told me she was busy doing family things. I wondered if this were really true or had she been hanging out with them secretly, without telling me?

I wasn't allowed to have a Facebook account so I had no idea who Millie's Facebook friends were and I'd never really thought about it before. But now that I knew, it explained her strange behavior over the last couple of weeks.

What hurt the most was that she hadn't told me. Of course Millie had the right to hang out with whomever she wanted. But I thought that we were best friends and surely, she'd be happy to include me.

And how could she want to be friends with Sara Hamilton anyway? How could she even consider her as a friend? That girl is an evil bully and Millie knows it!

"What's wrong, Julia? You look like you've seen a ghost!"

Millie's words caught me completely unaware and I looked up to see her standing in the doorway.

"Are you sick?" she asked with concern. "What's the matter?"

Millie appeared to be so genuine, that I quickly convinced myself I had made a mistake and that there was a perfectly good explanation. Still feeling guilty about invading her privacy, I haltingly replied, "Oh, I'm okay. How are you?"

Then I saw her gaze drop to her bed where her guitar lay haphazardly on top of her quilt. So I quickly added, "Your mom said I could play your guitar while I was waiting. I hope you don't mind."

"Oh that's fine," said Millie. "You can use it anytime. And sorry I'm late by the way. I got held up at the mall trying to find a present for my dad's birthday. It's so hard buying presents for someone who has everything!" she exclaimed.

I looked at her expectantly, waiting for the words that would explain the mystery. But instead she abruptly continued, "I don't know about you but I'm starving. Let's go and see if Mom has dinner ready!"

I followed her in silence down the stairs and picked at my meal. I had no appetite and all I really wanted to do was go home. Thankfully, Millie was feeling tired and after watching a movie on TV, we decided to have an early night and go to bed.

It was several hours later before I finally drifted off to sleep. Tossing and turning, I could not remove the vision from my mind of Millie and her new friends. I wondered what would happen at school on Monday and if our friendship would ever be the same again.

She's my friend...

Millie was waiting for me at the bus stop on Monday morning as usual. It was as if nothing had happened. Maybe I was wrong, I thought to myself. Maybe Millie did just go shopping for her dad's present. I could be blowing the whole thing out of proportion and making a problem when there really wasn't one.

I didn't know what I should do. I wanted to confront Millie and ask her about what I had seen on her Facebook page but I just couldn't bring myself to tell her that I had looked without her permission. I still felt so guilty over that and was at a loss as to what I should do.

Feeling too upset to stay, I had left Millie's early the day before, using the excuse that I wasn't feeling that great and still had homework to finish. But now I was convinced that I had it all wrong.

We headed up to class to find Mrs. Jackson collecting our homework assignments. Some people still hadn't completed theirs and others were complaining about how difficult it had been. Feeling confident, I handed mine to her and smiled, the vision of that A flashing through my mind.

Just then, I heard someone call out from the back of the room. "Hey Millie, do you want to hang out with us during lunch break today?"

Millie and I both turned around to find out who the question had come from. With total dismay, I could see Sara Hamilton, smiling broadly in our direction. Glancing briefly at Millie, who suddenly seemed very flustered, I opened my desk and pulled out my Math book, pretending that I wanted to start work.

My mind was spinning. "What's going on? Has Millie really become friends with Sara? This can't be happening!" a frightened voice inside my head screamed.

When the lunch bell finally rang, everyone raced out the door, keen to get to their favorite spots. Millie and I sat down in our usual place and began eating. After a few minutes of awkward silence, Millie stood and said, "I need to go to the bathroom. I'll be back in a few minutes."

I sat there alone, waiting for her to return. After a while, I gave up and headed for the library with some other friends who had been sitting nearby. It's better than sitting on my own, I thought to myself, wondering where Millie had got to.

I hadn't bothered looking for her because deep down, I knew where she would be. In the spot with the cool group, where they always hung out and there was no way I could bring myself to join her. That would be too humiliating.

Back in class, I whispered, "Millie…where did you get to during lunch break?"

"I was just talking to Harry and his friends," she replied in an off-handed manner. "They called me over, and then I couldn't find you."

"Enough of that chatter, girls!" exclaimed Mrs. Jackson. "Recess is over; it's time to get on with your work."

Millie put her head down and avoided eye contact. As much as I tried, I could not focus on the English task we'd been asked to complete. I felt really upset and didn't know what to do.

After school, Millie said a quick goodbye and left, saying that she'd see me at school the next day. I boarded the bus and headed to my usual seat near the back. I sat down and looked sadly out the window, thinking about Millie's words earlier.

It's true…Millie is hanging out with that group and I'm sure she was with them at the mall on Saturday as well; so much for being my best friend!

Just as I started to think about Harry Robinson, and the possibility of him liking Millie, Blake Jansen flopped down on the seat next to me. "Hey," he said. "What's up with you today? You look like the world is coming to an end!"

Gratefully I looked up at Blake, so glad to see his friendly face. He was a person who always seemed happy and positive. I think that's why I enjoyed his company so much.

And he didn't strut around, making out he was the best at everything, although he could if he wanted to. He was one of those kids who seemed to be good at everything – good at school work, good at sport; he had made the regional football team and he was also a really good drummer. Then to top it all off, he was good looking as well!

I sat back and started to think differently about Blake. The thought of the mysterious dream book also entered my mind. I must read it again tonight, I decided; before Mom has to return it to her friend. Blake's positive personality made me completely forget about my problems with Millie and her new friends. I even stopped thinking about Harry. And when Blake invited me over to his house to hang out on the weekend, I eagerly accepted.

At least I have that to look forward to I thought to myself as I hopped off the bus and waved goodbye to Blake. Then I headed on up to my bedroom, keen to read my favorite new book one more time.

The fight...

It was the loud yelling that woke me. I'd been in a deep sleep, dreaming of Millie and Harry Robinson holding hands and smiling into each other's eyes. And just as they were about to kiss, I woke with a huge start.

At first I didn't know where I was or what was happening, but then the sound of my mother's voice shook me back to consciousness. My parents had been fighting a lot lately, but something in Mom's voice forced me out of bed and made me race for my bedroom door. My throat felt tight with fear as I threw the door open. It was suddenly deadly quiet and I didn't know what I would find.

As I headed into the kitchen, the first thing I noticed was the mess on the worn floorboards. What appeared to be a broken serving dish and the remains of an uneaten meal lay scattered across the bench top and was dripping onto the floor below.

There was no sign of my parents anywhere! That was when I started to panic. Nervously, I opened the front door and looked out onto the empty driveway where our car had been parked earlier that evening. Our garage was so full of junk, that we hadn't been able to fit our car in there for as long as I could remember. It was then I spotted my mother, hunched over on the bottom step, her head buried deep in her lap. As I quickly approached her, I could hear the soft sound of her quiet sobbing and I wrapped my arms around her shaking shoulders.

"Mom!" I stammered. "Are you alright? Where's Dad? What happened?"

"Oh Julia, he was so angry!" she sobbed. "I've never seen

him like that before. I don't know if he's coming back!"

"But what happened tonight? Why is there such a mess in the kitchen?" I questioned, fear gripping the pit of my stomach.

"He went into a rage! He threw his dinner on the floor, ran out the door and drove off.

I think your father needs help, Julia! I don't know what to do!" Mom was almost hysterical.

I gently coaxed her back into the house. She was a mess. They'd been fighting more and more but it had never been this bad before. Tonight I felt like I was the parent. I made her a cup of tea and sat down with her while she drank it. I shook my head at the thought of my brother still sound asleep in his bed. A bomb could literally go off and I'm sure it wouldn't wake him. He almost went into a coma when he went to sleep. It constantly amazed me.

"What happened, Mom?" I asked her gently. "I've never seen or heard of Dad getting into such a state before! What caused him to get so angry?"

"He said it's all my fault!" she sobbed. "He said that he can't stand living with me anymore. Then he got really angry and left. What am I going to do?"

I sat there frantically worrying about my parents and the way they've been acting with each other lately. That was another thing that I was envious of Millie for. Her parents always seemed so happy. I never heard a raised voice in her house, everyone seemed to get on well and her Mom never nagged Millie or her brother.

Millie complains about her parents sometimes, but I always tell her that she doesn't know how good she has it. Secretly, I think that my parents are so worried about money problems, that it makes them fight; whereas, Millie's parents don't have to deal with that issue. I know that money doesn't buy happiness, but it certainly seems to help sometimes.

I sat comforting my mom, feeling closer to her than I had in ages. We talked about good things and bad things but the best part was that we were actually talking. I used to be so close to my mom and I really missed the special times we always shared together.

Eventually, I coaxed her back into bed, hoping more than anything that Dad would return by the morning and everything would be okay.

How to Make Your Dreams Come True! The tattered brown cover caught my eye as I climbed back into bed. Even though I was exhausted and terribly worried, I switched on my bedside lamp and continued reading from where I had left off before going to sleep.

A couple of hours later, I turned the last page and read and reread the final paragraph, taking in the meaning of the words in front of me…Dream, Believe and Achieve. With a positive mindset and belief in yourself and your dreams, anything is possible.

With those words foremost in my mind, I turned off the light and went to sleep.

Conflict...

Tiptoeing downstairs the next morning, I silently approached the kitchen. I was desperately hoping to see my dad in his usual spot, reading the morning paper before leaving for work. But my heart sank at the sight of my mother sitting alone at the kitchen bench.

Hearing me approach, she looked up, a worried frown visible on her face. In answer to my unspoken question, her words broke the still silence, "He came back in the middle of the night and left again for work very early this morning. We hardly spoke. But at least he did say that he'll be back at his usual time late this afternoon."

I breathed a huge sigh of relief and when I sat down next to her, I remembered what was clasped firmly in my hand. "Mom, I want you to promise me that you'll read this!" I said adamantly, placing the book down on the bench top in front of her, the gold swirly letters of the title glowing mysteriously from the cover.

"What is it, Julia?" she asked. "I have a lot on my mind at the moment. And sitting down to read isn't a top priority right now."

"Mom, this isn't just any book! I've never read anything like this before and I really think that you should read it too." I pleaded with her, wanting more than anything for her to just listen to me.

"I don't think that it was a coincidence your friend dropped in and left this book for you. I really think that we were both meant to read it. Just put aside some time and promise me that you'll at least have a look at it."

There was probably something in my tone that made her agree. Reluctantly she nodded her head and said that she would make an effort to read some of it before leaving for work at midday.

Feeling slightly relieved, I quickly ate some breakfast and raced for the shower before my brother got there before me.

He was still asleep in bed, blissfully unaware of what had happened the night before. He's probably dreaming of Lily, I smirked to myself, and doesn't want to wake up.

I sneaked quickly into the bathroom, before he woke and created a scene about needing it first. Then headed out to the bus stop, where I waited for the bus, deep in thought. I was feeling a little concerned about going to school and facing Millie, really not sure what her reaction would be.

Determined to stay positive though, I boarded the bus, grabbed a seat up the back and focused on my parents being able to sort things out. They have had plenty of arguments before but I'd never seen Dad behave the way that Mom described. That was really scary and I tried to put the terrible image out of my mind.

As the bus pulled up in front of the school, I looked apprehensively out the window for the familiar sight of Millie, waiting for me to arrive. But she was nowhere to be seen. My heart dropped and with my eyes downcast, I made my way to our classroom and sat down quietly at my desk, waiting for the bell to ring.

Millie seemed to appear from nowhere. I turned my head and there she was sitting at her desk next to me. "Hey Julia!" she said, smiling happily. "How are you?"

"Good thanks," I replied. "Were you running late this morning?"

"Yeah, I was in the biggest rush. I never thought I'd get here!" she explained as she got out her books ready to start work.

Reassured by her friendly manner, I decided to ask her if we could maybe hang out after school one afternoon during the week. But then Mrs. Jackson dropped a collection of papers upside down on our desks. I realized it was our Math assignments and I nervously turned mine over.

The big red A+ stood out clearly in the top right hand corner, along with Mrs. Jackson's neatly written comment...Excellent work, Julia. A fabulous effort!

I was sure that the beaming smile that had spread across my face was an exact replica of the one I had previously been picturing in my mind.

"Oh my gosh!" I exclaimed ecstatically. "I've never achieved an A in Math before, yet alone an A+. I can't believe it!"

Millie looked down with disgust at the C on her assignment. She is normally an all-round A student and it was clear that she was not happy.

"Oh whatever!" Millie rolled her eyes skyward. "It's just a stupid Math assignment. I was too busy on the weekend to spend much time on it. Who cares anyway?"

Her mouth set in a firm line, she then proceeded to get on with the work that Mrs. Jackson had put on the board. She was acting as though she wasn't bothered about the C, but it was plainly obvious that she was upset. She was definitely not used to scoring low marks. Clearly though, she didn't want to talk, so we silently continued our work.

When the bell rang for morning recess later that morning, without a word, Millie left her desk and was out the door before I could barely even blink. The pleasure I had felt earlier at the sight of the A+ on my homework had completely disappeared.

That's mean, Millie!!

Miserably, I wandered down the stairs looking for some other friends to hang out with. The trouble with having one best friend is that if you have a falling out, then you're left on your own.

Thankfully though, there are some nice girls in our class who were more than happy for me to join them. I was so grateful that at least I didn't have to be a total loner, although it was a huge effort to try to take part in their conversation.

My earlier hope of Millie and I sorting things out was obviously something that was not going to happen. Her friendliness when she had arrived in class was all fake. I could see that now.

I heard some raucous laughter coming from nearby and stole a glance in that direction. It was Sara Hamilton and her group of friends, cracking up over some joke or another, I guessed. And Millie, who was sitting amongst them, seemed to be the center of attention. Laughing and joking, they appeared to be having heaps of fun and right by Millie's side was Harry Robinson. His long blonde fringe was flicked to one side and his beautiful blue eyes were focused completely on Millie.

The familiar pangs of jealousy hit me with a thud and I rushed to the bathroom in tears. So much for making my dreams come true. What a load of garbage; and what a waste of time convincing my Mom to read that dream book. I'll probably get home and my parents will have split up.

These were the thoughts racing through my mind when I suddenly heard people approaching. I quickly splashed water over my tear stained face, not wanting anyone to see that I was upset. Then the sound of a familiar voice made me gasp, "I love hanging out with you guys. It's so much more fun than being with Julia!"

Horrified, I looked towards Millie who suddenly realized that I'd overheard her conversation. The look of guilt was clearly visible on her face and as I rushed past her, speechless, I couldn't help but notice Sara's cold menacing eyes and smug look of victory.

Back in class, my head was spinning. There was no way that I could even look at Millie. Without making a scene, I moved my desk as far away from hers as possible. Then I put my head down, pretending to do some work but concentrated with all my might on preventing the tears from falling. As Sara walked past on her way to her desk, I couldn't help but notice her confident smirk.

"No!" a voice screamed inside my head. "You cannot let her get to you!" Memories of her terrible bullying still haunted me and I knew that I would have to be really strong to ensure it didn't happen all over again.

Being confident and assertive was the only way I'd been able to overcome all the problems I'd had with Sara in the past. Deep in my heart I knew that. So with a huge amount of effort, I gathered all my strength, took a deep breath and got on with my work, pretending that I was not bothered whatsoever.

I could not let them see that I was upset. That would only allow Sara to regain her power over me and I was determined that I would never be bullied like that again. I had to stay strong and believe that Millie would eventually find out who her true friend was. With a determination I didn't know I possessed, I put all thoughts of Millie and her new friends out of my mind and got on with my school work.

Turning it around...

Dinner that night was very uncomfortable. I could feel the tension between Mom and Dad and picked at my food quietly. I had absolutely no appetite and was hoping to be excused from the table as quickly as possible.

Thankfully Matt was his usual loud and chatty self. Clearly oblivious to the awkward silence around him, he prattled on about some kid at school who is an awesome basketball player and has been selected to play in a regional tournament.

Matt has a huge passion for basketball and spends most of his spare time at the nearby courts, practicing and playing in the local competition. Mom isn't happy about all the time he spends there, but Dad keeps reassuring her that it's better for him to be active than sitting at home on the computer.

Finally, I was allowed to be excused and as it was Matt's turn to do the dishes, I was able to sneak on up to my bedroom.

About an hour later as I sat at my desk staring blankly at my homework, I heard a quiet knock. "Come in," I called and Mom hesitatingly peeked her head around the door.

"Sorry to interrupt your homework, darling" she said gently. "Is it okay if I come in?"

"Yes, of course," I replied, and looked up at her not sure what to expect.

"I read quite a bit of that book today," she said. "I actually became so engrossed that I forgot the time and was nearly late for work."

I looked at my mother, waiting for her to continue. I had not anticipated this.

Sitting down on my bed, she exclaimed, "Julia, you're right! It's a fabulous book and something that I think I should have read a long time ago!"

"Yes, but I don't know if what they talk about in that book can really happen," I said in a defiant manner. "So many things seem to be going wrong at the moment – it's pretty obvious that the stuff they mention doesn't work."

"It's all about your attitude, Julia. Thinking negative thoughts will only give you a negative response," she continued. "You need to stay positive and focus on the things that you want to happen, rather than constantly worrying about what you don't want to happen."

"Do you understand, sweetheart?"

"Yes, of course I understand," I scoffed rudely. I couldn't believe that she was now lecturing me on the book that I had encouraged her to read. "I've been trying so hard to stay positive but everything is going wrong! Like I told you, it doesn't work!"

I knew that I was reacting to everything that had happened; my problems at school with Millie and Sara, Harry Robinson taking a sudden interest in Millie and Mom and Dad on the verge of splitting up. How on earth was I supposed to be positive when I had all that going on around me?

I sat there sulking miserably. It was all just too hard and it wasn't fair! First I lose my best friend and then my parents decide to split up. Why is this happening when all I've been trying to do is to be positive and make my dreams come true? I certainly wasn't hoping for negative stuff to happen, that's for sure.

"I know it can be very difficult to keep a positive mindset," said Mom. "But the secret is to try your hardest to really believe that everything will work out and it usually does."

"How come you're suddenly acting like this?" I asked her. "I've never heard you talk this way before."

"I should have taken these ideas on board a long time ago," she sighed. "I know that I'm pretty much to blame for your Dad's reaction last night. I've been such a negative presence in this house for a long time now. But reading the dream book today, has made me realize that I have so much to be grateful for! I have a beautiful loving husband who tries to do his best and two wonderful children who I should be very proud of."

I sat there staring at my mother in disbelief. Who was this person? I couldn't remember her ever talking this way before!

"Reading what I did today, really opened my eyes and now I can see that I've been making a huge mistake. But it's up to me to change that. Since dinner tonight, your father and I have been talking and really listening to each other. I think that it's the closest we have been in a long time! I really believe that everything will be ok between us, Julia. You don't have to worry."

Completely taken aback by my mother's words, I sat staring into space for a few moments. Then unexpectedly, something very important that I had totally forgotten about abruptly popped into my mind.

"I completely forgot to mention it, but there is one positive thing that has happened to me since reading the dream book."

"Really?" she asked. "What is it?"

"We got our Math assignment back today. I didn't tell you but I worked really hard on it and focused on getting an A. And guess what! I actually got an A+! I've never done that well in Math before – it was like a miracle!" I exclaimed loudly, my energy level taking a sudden shift.

"Julia, that is so wonderful!" The pleased look on my mother's face really lifted my spirits but then without any warning whatsoever, I burst into tears.

Changing...

"Julia, it's going to be okay!"

My mother hugged me and stroked my hair the way she used to when I was little. I honestly couldn't remember the last time I had hugged my mother. But it felt so good.

It was what I needed just then; some reassurance that everything was going to work out. And for the first time in ages, I poured out all my problems. I told her all about Millie and how upset I was. I told her that I was scared to go to school the following day and I told her about how important I had always thought it was to be accepted by the cool group.

It felt so good to actually be talking to her about everything that was bothering me. And the best part was, she sat and listened without being critical, or telling me I was being silly, or that I should just grow up and get over it.

Rather than doing any of these things, Mom gave me some advice. And I really think that it's the best advice that she has ever given me.

"Julia," she said kindly but firmly, "See in your mind what you want to happen, believe that it will happen and just stay positive. You'll be amazed at the miracles you can create!"

It was like my mother was a different person. But I was so glad at that moment that she was my mother. And I was so very grateful to her friend for lending us her dream book. What a gift and what a huge difference it had made already.

Mom said goodnight and left me to my thoughts. It took me a while to fall asleep but the visions floating around in my head were the dreams that I was determined would come true.

So sorry…

I can't say that it was easy, but I managed to get through the following week at school. I continued to sit in the same spot in class that I always had, right by Millie. I talked briefly to her, but wasn't mean or nasty or cruel in any way.

During lunch breaks, I hung out with the other girls who had welcomed me into their group. I occasionally watched Millie becoming more and more a part of the "cool" kids' group. And while I didn't like what I saw, I didn't criticize or comment.

I continued to focus on eventually regaining my friendship with Millie. But I completely changed my mind about Harry Robinson and the group Millie was hanging out with. And I cursed myself for even having considered being friends with them, especially when Sara Hamilton was involved.

Finally though, it was the weekend, and I went to Blake's house as planned. I had really been looking forward to that and we'd organized that we would spend time in his dad's music studio as we both loved music so much.

Blake's dad is an awesome drummer but he also plays guitar and has several guitars lying around. I was so excited when he told me that as long as I was careful, I could have a play on one of them. He even taught me the chords to some popular songs and in no time at all, I was managing to play them reasonably well. He was very impressed with how quickly I learnt what he had taught me and that made me feel very proud.

For what seemed like several hours, Blake played his drums, while I strummed chords on his dad's guitar. It was the most fun that I'd had in ages.

We decided that we'd hang out again the following weekend. I felt so grateful to have Blake for a friend. And already, I couldn't wait to get together again in his dad's studio. Finally it was time for me to leave and with a reluctant goodbye, I headed home.

As I walked in my front door later that afternoon, I could hear the telephone ringing. Although I rushed to answer it, by the time I had picked it up and said hello, the person calling had hung up. Heading into the kitchen for a quick snack before dinner, I heard the phone ring again. The familiar voice on the other end was so unexpected, that I stood still with shock.

"Julia! Please don't hang up on me!" It took me a moment to realize that Millie was crying. "Can I please come over?" she begged. "I need to talk to you!"

I could hear in her voice that she was very upset and although my immediate reaction was to say that I was busy, I quietly agreed.

With anxious anticipation, I waited by the front door, not knowing what to expect. Why did she want to visit me all of a sudden and why was she so upset? I started to panic that something very bad may have happened. But why come to me about it? These questions raced through my mind as I waited worriedly for her to arrive.

At the sound of the bell, I opened the door and Millie burst in, tears streaming down her face.

"Julia, I'm so sorry," she cried. "Will you ever forgive me?"

Mouth agape, I stood looking at her, overcome with shock at her words.

"Come up to my room," I replied. "And tell me what's going

on."

"They were so mean to me," she sobbed as she sat down on my bed. "They invited me to hang out with them at the mall today and when I got there, they just ignored me."

"Who are you talking about, Millie?" I asked, even though I was sure that I knew the answer.

"Sara and Harry and all their friends," Millie cried. "At first, they wouldn't even talk to me and then they started making fun of me. They were whispering to each other and being so mean. It was humiliating! I didn't know what to do!"

"I thought Harry liked me," she sobbed once more. "But he's the meanest of them all! He thinks he's so cool and just puts everyone down. And all they do is gossip about everyone at school and make up lies. It's horrible!"

I sat there looking at Millie sympathetically. I really did feel sorry for her. It wasn't her fault that she had been sucked in by them. It could easily have been me. I had originally wanted to hang out with them too. I thought that being with them would make me cool, but they're not genuine friends at all. And I couldn't believe that I'd been so obsessed with

Harry either. He seemed to be the biggest jerk of them all!

"Julia, will you please forgive me?" Millie begged.

"You're my best friend and you always will be! I'm really sorry that I was so mean to you. I don't deserve to have you as my friend, but please say you'll forgive me!"

All the terrible memories and hurtful moments thinking I had lost my closest friend, disappeared in an instant. And within minutes, Millie and I were back to being best friends again.

Just like that, out of the blue, another of my dreams had come true.

I had my best friend back. And as well, it had seemed that over the past week my parents were getting on better than ever. What more could I ask for!

A guitar...

Millie ended up sleeping over at my house. We spent hours in my room, painting our fingernails and toenails, listening to music and making up new dance moves. Millie braided my hair; she's so good at braiding. I don't know how she does it.

We chatted and laughed so much that Mom came in to find out what was so amusing. It was like old times and I was absolutely overjoyed to have Millie back in my life as my best friend.

The next day, we decided to head over to her house as I was so desperate to have another turn of her beautiful guitar. However, when we arrived, she told me to go on up to her room because she needed a few minutes to talk with her mother.

I didn't think anything of it, just raced up to her room and carefully took her guitar from its case. Sitting on her bed, her guitar in my hands, I didn't feel I could possibly be any happier.

About 20 minutes passed and then Millie and her mom walked in; the looks on their faces so serious that I started to panic, thinking something must be terribly wrong.

"Julia," Millie said in a grave tone. "We have something to tell you!"

My stomach turned in knots. I had no idea what to expect. "What's wrong?" I exclaimed.

Then Millie laughed out loud, "Absolutely nothing; I actually have some really good news."

"Don't scare me like that!" I replied. "I thought something really bad had happened!"

I had no idea what she was going to say, but the anxiety in the pit of my stomach quickly turned to excited anticipation.

In a rush, her words spilled out, "I checked with Mom and she said that it's fine for you to borrow my guitar. You can use it for as long as you like!"

The grin on Millie's face could not have been any wider if she had tried.

I looked at her in total disbelief. Then I looked at her mom and back at Millie again. "What do you mean?" I asked. "It's your brand new guitar. I don't understand."

"Millie really isn't interested in learning how to play the guitar, Julia. She's had it a few weeks now and hasn't practiced once," Mrs. Spencer explained gently. "I had a feeling that this would happen but she insisted that she wanted to learn how to play. I'd rather see it being used than put away in a cupboard. And I know that you'll look after it."

"But I couldn't possibly," I stammered.

"It's obvious to me, that you're very keen to learn," she continued, "We'd love you to have the opportunity. You've been such a good friend to Millie and it's something she would like to do for you. And you never know, watching you learn might inspire her to take it up again. In the meantime, it's yours to borrow."

I looked from Mrs. Spencer back to Millie once more.

"You have a natural gift, Julia. Everyone can see that." Millie was talking excitedly and it was clear that this was what she wanted.

"You're the one who should definitely be learning how to play, not me. I don't have a musical bone in my body."

Mrs. Spencer left us to talk alone. Millie sat down on her bed next to me and continued sincerely, "I only wanted it so I could fit in with those kids at school. But I don't want to have anything to do with them anymore. And who knows? Your birthday is coming up. When your parents see how keen you are, they might even buy you a guitar of your own."

I was speechless. I did not know what to say. The tears that rolled down my cheeks right then, were not from sadness. They were tears of joy.

Thank you, Millie!

I had my best friend back. My best friend who was the most generous person in the entire world and she was giving me the most wonderful gift that I could ever imagine. Right then, I knew that it wasn't the guitar that I was so grateful for, but Millie's friendship. I truly did have a best friend and felt that I was the luckiest girl on the planet!

Back in my own bedroom that night, I sat with the beautiful, shiny, pink, electric guitar in my hands, strumming some new chords that I had been practicing all afternoon. Thank goodness for YouTube and the beginner lessons that I had found. And thank goodness for my friend Millie!

Mom simply smiled at me, a knowing look in her eyes when she heard what Millie and Mrs. Spencer had said. Yes, my dreams were coming true. It was like a miracle and I felt more grateful than ever.

I could hear Mom and Dad downstairs laughing together. That alone was music to my ears. It was a sound that I hadn't heard coming from them in such a long time.

For the first time in weeks, I really looked forward to going to school the following day. I wondered what wonderful things lay ahead.

It's all happening...

Millie and I spent our lunch breaks with the lovely group of girls who I had been hanging out with over the previous couple of weeks. It was fun being part of a big group and especially because they were such genuinely nice girls.

On several occasions, I noticed Sara, Harry and their friends looking in our direction and laughing, obviously about us. But we just chose to ignore them and focus on the friends we wanted to be with.

This proved to work because after a while the group who we didn't think of as "cool" anymore seemed to lose interest in us and not bother us whatsoever, which was great. Once more, school was a fun place to be.

Then without warning, one afternoon just after we had come back from our lunch break, Mr. Casey the guitar teacher arrived at our classroom door. Totally unexpectedly, he asked Mrs. Jackson if he could speak with me. I made my way to the doorway where he was standing, wondering what on earth he could want. The words that came out of his mouth caught me completely by surprise.

"Julia, I've heard that you're very keen to learn how to play the guitar," he queried.

"Um, yes," I replied hesitatingly. "I'd love to learn but my parents really can't afford lessons right now. So I've just been trying to teach myself by watching YouTube videos."

"Well, Blake Jansen's dad is a friend of mine. He's a very good musician and I respect his opinion. When I was speaking to him on the phone last night, he mentioned that you have a natural gift for guitar. He thinks you're very talented! So I'd like to offer you a scholarship and that way you can have free lessons for the rest of the year."

I looked at him confused. I wasn't sure that I fully grasped what he was saying.

"This is something that I've decided to introduce to the school music program this year," he continued.

"I have a couple of other kids who have already started on a scholarship program with me." He looked at me expectantly, waiting for my reply.

"Oh my gosh!" as the full meaning of what he was saying started to sink in, I could barely contain my excitement. "That would be so awesome!"

The delight I felt at that moment was indescribable. I felt like jumping up and down with joy.

"Well you'll have to get your parents' permission first," he explained. "Go home and talk to them about it tonight and if it's okay with them, bring this completed permission note back to me tomorrow. Then we can arrange a suitable time for your lessons."

He handed me the note as I stood there, desperately wanting to run inside and tell Millie the exciting news.

"But there's one condition," he stated firmly.

"Okay," I replied warily. "What's that?"

"To be eligible for a scholarship, you must commit to regular practice. It's all written in the note. It's kind of like a contract that you actually need to sign as well as your parents. I only offer scholarships to students who are willing to be committed; only those who agree to regular attendance and at least 5 hours of practice each week."

"Oh, that's fine!" I replied, feeling relieved, "That won't be a problem at all. Do you think I could start lessons tomorrow?"

He smiled widely, obviously pleased with my eager response. "Get the permission note signed first and I'll talk to you tomorrow."

"This is so exciting, Mr. Casey. Thank you so much!" I was bouncing up and down on the spot, overcome with joy.

Finally he left and I was able to race back to my desk, glad that the bell was almost due to ring so I could share my incredible news with Millie.

I also couldn't wait to get on the bus and speak with Blake. I had so much to thank him and his dad for.

This was totally amazing. As I boarded the bus that afternoon, the thought occurred to me that my dreams were actually all coming true. I had so much to be grateful for. I remembered that was one of the main principles explained in the dream book...by being grateful for all the wonderful things that you already have in your life, so much more will come to you that you can also be grateful for.

Yes, gratitude was a huge part of making your dreams a reality. And at that moment, I felt as though I would have to be the most grateful girl alive.

Happiness...

My first lesson with Mr. Casey was unbelievable. I did not want it to end! And as soon as I walked into the house that afternoon, I headed straight up to my room to practice.

"The only problem I can see here," said Mom, a slight frown appearing on her face, "is that you'll spend so much time playing guitar, you'll have no time for your homework."

"Mom!" I said, smiling broadly, "I promise that I'll stay on top of my school work." And as an afterthought, I jumped up from where I had been sitting, guitar still in my hands, and gave her a big hug. "Thank you so much for letting me learn how to play! I just love it!"

"I can see that," she replied with a grin. "And I'm very impressed to see you learning so fast!"

"So am I!" exclaimed Matt, as he walked past my bedroom door. "I hate to say this, but sis, you're actually pretty good!"

Coming from my brother, that was the compliment of the century.

I felt so happy. It was amazing how much things in our household had changed. Matt was even on his way out to meet his girlfriend Lily, with the approval of Mom and Dad. Now that was definitely a miracle!

Completely content, I adjusted the volume on my amplifier slightly, and continued playing the latest new song that I had learnt. I have so much to be grateful for I thought to myself as I eventually put the guitar carefully back in its case, deciding that it was time to get stuck into my homework.

I sat down at my desk, school books in front of me, and considered the events that had taken place over the past few weeks. Life had completely turned around for my entire family and all because of a very special book that had been left for us to read.

"Thank goodness I decided to pick that book up," I smiled contentedly to myself as I concentrated happily on my Math.

My dream came true...

"Julia, how would you like to be in a band?" Mr. Casey asked one afternoon at the end of my lesson. The answer to that question was completely obvious by the look on my face.

"I'm organizing a couple of bands for kids who are interested and I thought that you'd be great as one of the guitarists."

"That would be the most amazing thing ever!" I exclaimed. And then a moment later I asked, "Do you have any drummers in mind?"

With a smile, he replied, "I thought that Blake Jansen would be a good choice."

As I boarded the bus that afternoon, I was unable to remove the beaming smile that was spread across my face. Flopping down in the seat that Blake always saved for me, I said with a grin, "Mr. Casey is forming a band. And guess who he has asked to be the guitarist!"

"Julia!" he exclaimed. "It's you, isn't it?" His beautiful smiling face made my heart melt.

"And guess who he would like to have as the drummer?" I stared directly at him.

"Me?" he questioned hopefully.

"Well who else would it be?" I teased.

"Oh, that is sooo cool!"

"I know," I replied. "It's a dream come true!"

When he held my hand right then, the flutter that ran down my spine made me completely breathless.

"Julia," he said, "Do you want to go out with me? I mean, really go out – like on a date?"

With absolutely no hesitation at all, I replied, "I'd love to Blake. That would be awesome!"

Then we sat silently side by side, hands locked together wishing that our bus ride home would last forever.

Read all about Julia's ongoing adventures in the next book in the series and find out what is in store for Julia and her friends...

This book continues the ongoing adventures of Julia Jones and is filled with suspense, excitement and very special friendships. There is also one friendship in particular that Julia dreams of.
But not everything goes according to plan, especially when Sara decides to take control. Julia is then forced to create the reality she wants in her life by trying to make things happen the way she had hoped.
A heart-warming and inspiring story that all young girls are sure to relate to and enjoy.

Thank you for reading my book. If you liked it could you please leave a review?
Katrina

***

Please Like our Facebook page

to keep updated on the release date for each new book in the series...

www.facebook.com/JuliaJonesDiary

and follow us on Instagram:

@juliajonesdiary

Announcing a New Series!

Find out what lies ahead for Julia and all her friends in a brand new series...

Mind Reader – Book 1: My New Life

OUT NOW!!

This book introduces Emmie, a girl who unexpectedly arrives in Carindale and meets Millie. But Emmie has a secret, a secret that must remain hidden at all costs.
What happens to Julia, Blake, Sara and all the others and how does Emmie's sudden appearance impact Julia and her friends?

This fabulous new series continues the story of Julia Jones but has a whole new twist, one that all Julia Jones' Diary fans are sure to enjoy.

Announcing a New Series!

Exciting News! Katrina Kahler has continued to tell the story of Julia Jones - 3 years on - yes, the Teenage Years. Julia is older, but is she wiser? Whatever happened to Blake and Sara?

Grab the first new book in the series now! You'll love it!

Julia Jones – The Teenage years

Book 1: 'Falling Apart'

Out NOW!

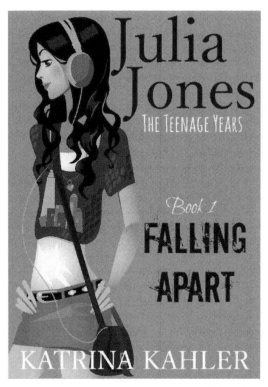

Here are some more books that you're sure to love!

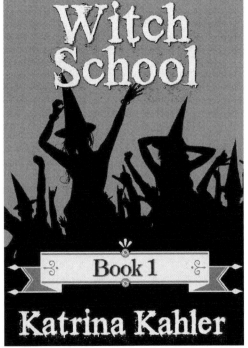

***

Follow Julia Jones on Instagram @juliajonesdiary

And be sure to visit...

http://diaryofanalmostcoolgirl.com/

This is where you'll find all the bestselling books for kids!

Printed in Great Britain
by Amazon